The Red Thread

An Adoption Fairy Tale

by Grace Lin

ALBERT WHITMAN & COMPANY, MORTON GROVE, ILLINOIS

This book is dedicated to all children adopted, the parents
who loved them but could not keep them, and
the parents who traveled far to find them.

With special thanks to the LaCroix-Pan Family,
the Congdon Girls, and the Keane-D'Alessandro Family.

Library of Congress Cataloging-in-Publication Data

Lin, Grace.
The red thread : an adoption fairy tale / written and illustrated by Grace Lin.
p. cm.
Summary: A sad king and queen find joy and happiness after a mysterious red thread leads them to a baby waiting to be adopted.
ISBN 10: 0-8075-6922-4 (hardcover)
ISBN 13: 978-0-8075-6922-1 (hardcover)
[1. Adoption—Fiction. 2. Fairy tales.] I. Title.
PZ8.L6215Re 2007 [E]—dc22 2007001526

The design is by Carol Gildar.

For more information about Albert Whitman & Company,
please visit our web site at www.albertwhitman.com.

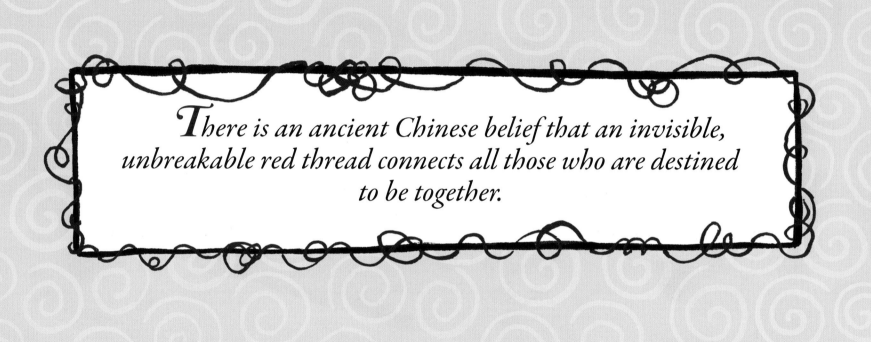

There is an ancient Chinese belief that an invisible, unbreakable red thread connects all those who are destined to be together.

"This story again? You've heard it a hundred times. Are you sure? Okay, I'll read it."

Once a king and queen ruled over a magnificent kingdom. Their subjects loved them, their castle shone like the sun, and there was never any famine or drought. They knew they were very lucky.

Yet, something was missing.

One morning the queen woke up with a pain in her heart. It was a steady ache that filled her with sadness.

"I have a pain in my heart," she said to the king. "It is a hurt that will not leave."

"I feel it, too," the king said. "It feels as if my heart is tearing in two."

So the king and queen called in doctors and scientists, wise men and medicine women. The healers made them drink special teas, breathe in orange herbs, recite rhyming poetry, and wear metal bracelets, but nothing worked. The pain remained, and grew worse each day. The king and queen began to lose hope that their suffering would end.

One day an old peddler wheeled his cart of trinkets into the kingdom. Hearing about the king and queen's distress, he requested an audience.

"It's as I thought," the man said when he saw them. "There is a red thread being pulled from your hearts!"

"A red thread?" The queen gasped. "Where?"

"I see nothing," the king said.

"Try on my spectacles," the peddler said, holding out his wire frames. "You will see."

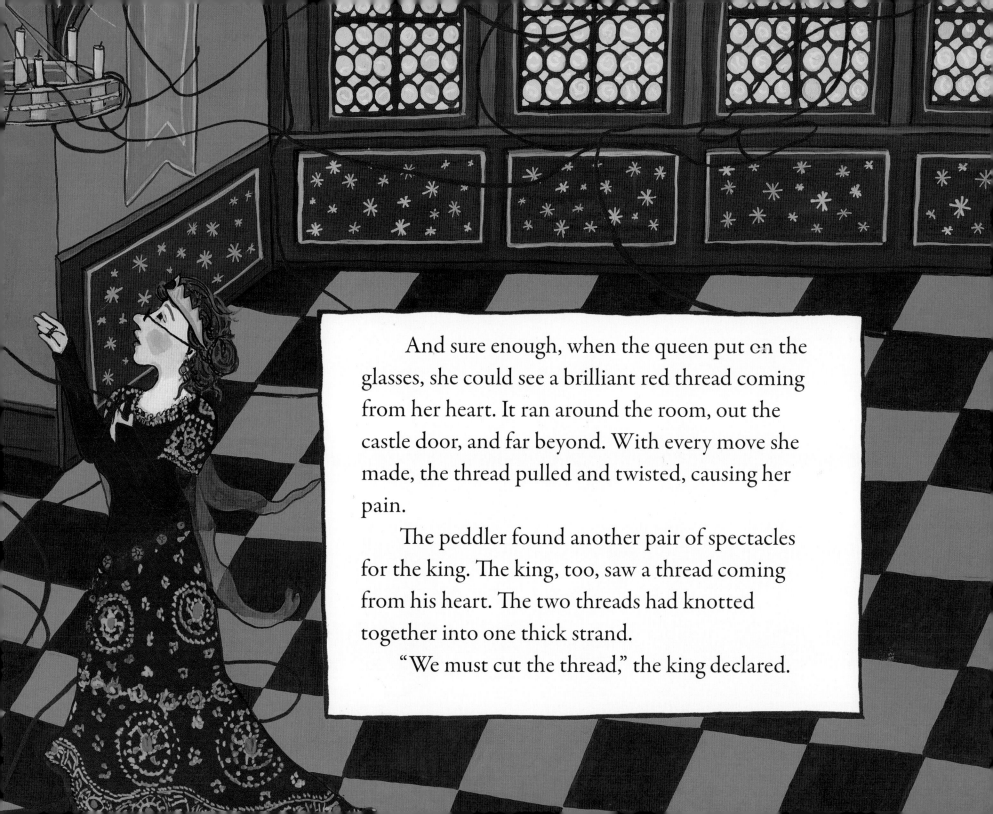

And sure enough, when the queen put on the glasses, she could see a brilliant red thread coming from her heart. It ran around the room, out the castle door, and far beyond. With every move she made, the thread pulled and twisted, causing her pain.

The peddler found another pair of spectacles for the king. The king, too, saw a thread coming from his heart. The two threads had knotted together into one thick strand.

"We must cut the thread," the king declared.

But no scissors, knife, or blade could cut the thread, any more than they could cut a beam from the moon.

"What should we do?" the queen cried in anguish.

"You will have to follow the thread," the peddler told them. "You both must find out who or what is pulling on the other end."

So the king and queen packed a basket of food and wine and left the kingdom in the care of the queen's sister. They followed the red thread out of the castle, and their subjects waved farewell.

Even though the king and the queen were sad to leave their kingdom, each step they took lessened the pain in their hearts.

It was a long and difficult journey. Snow fell, and sharp rocks made holes in their shoes. The king and queen shivered in the cold, and their fine clothes ripped from wear. Kind birds flew to help them untangle the thread from tree branches.

But the king and queen continued. They knew following the red thread was their only cure. As they traveled, the thread grew shorter and shorter.

Yet when the thread led them to the shore of a vast sea, they almost despaired. But the thread tugged at them, so they bought a boat and began to row.

With every stroke of the oars, they wondered what was pulling the thread.

Was it a ferocious beast or a cruel magician? What would they do when they met whatever was on the other end?

The king and queen finally reached the shore of a faraway land. The red thread guided them to a small village.

The people stared at them; they were so strange, with their clothes ripped to rags, hair tangled, and faces as pale as the moon. But the villagers smiled a greeting, for they were a friendly people.

The king and queen, however, took little notice of anyone. The end of the red thread was within their sight. They ran to a small bundle in front of an old house.

When they reached the bundle, both
stopped in amazement. Inside the bundle
was a baby!

She was laughing and playing and
tugging at the red threads tied around
each of her ankles. She looked up
at the king and queen
and smiled.

"Whose baby is this?" the queen asked. "Who does she belong to?"

Her words were strange to the villagers, who chattered a language that the king and queen could not understand. Finally a wrinkled elder pushed herself forward.

The elder's bespectacled eyes followed the short red threads connecting the king and queen to the baby. Her face broke into a broad smile.

"This baby," the old woman said, "belongs to you."

So the king and queen took the baby home to their castle, and she became the princess of the kingdom. They never felt the pain in their hearts again. Instead, they were filled with joy and happiness. They never found out how the red thread had connected them to their daughter, but they knew *why*. And that was all that mattered.

The king and queen searched for the old peddler to reward him for his help. But he had moved on to the next kingdom. He had heard the king and queen there were suffering from a pain in their hearts.

"Yes, it's our favorite story, too."